P9-DFU-200

## SHARE THIS BOOK WITH ALL YOUR FRIENDS!

Test your Disney knowledge
and find your Disney side!

**Disney PRESS**

LOS ANGELES • NEW YORK

Let's start with the basics.

## THIS BOOK BELONGS TO:

Brookly

NAME

DATE

## ??? YOU'RE FEELING?

## BEST FRIEND'S NAME:

casidy ♡ Haivly

### Favorite Disney Movie?

Sindrella

### Favorite Princess?

areolle

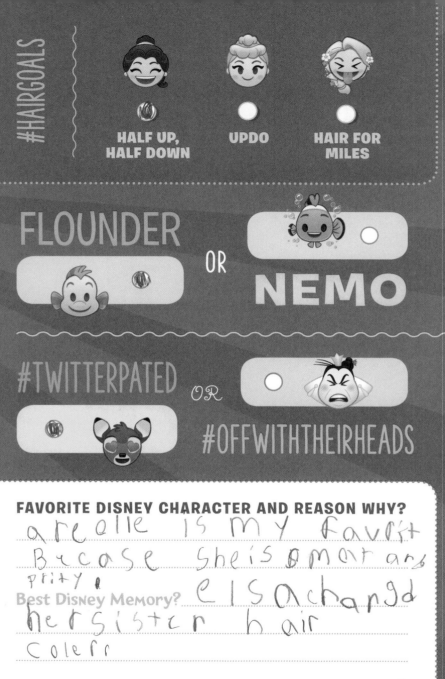

#HAIRGOALS

HALF UP, HALF DOWN

UPDO

HAIR FOR MILES

FLOUNDER

OR

NEMO

#TWITTERPATED

OR

#OFFWITHTHEIRHEADS

**FAVORITE DISNEY CHARACTER AND REASON WHY?**

areolle is my favrit Bcase she is smart and prity.

**Best Disney Memory?** elsa changd her sister hair colerr

3

# WOULD YOU RATHER . . .

We know you've dreamed of going on a date with your favorite Disney character, but which one? Would you traverse the night sky with Aladdin or dance the day away with Prince Phillip in the forest? Now is the time to make your choice.

## Would you rather BATTLE . . .

SCAR

MALEFICENT

Would you rather go on a *Date* with . . .

*Gaston*     *Hans*

Would you rather be
trapped on a deserted island with . . .

Stitch

Maui

Would you rather
go on an **ADVENTURE** with . . .

**Rapunzel**

**Ariel**

Would you rather be
TRAPPED in . . .

Wonderland

The Cave of Wonders

Would you rather be *granted a wish* from . . .

The
*Genie* ○

The
*Blue Fairy* 🖊️

Would you rather be BEST FRIENDS with . . .

PASCAL ○

DORY 🖊️

Would you rather have
the POWER of . . . 🖊️ MAMA ODIE

GRANDMOTHER WILLOW ○

Would you rather
## GO ON A MISSION with . . .

Buzz Lightyear

Judy Hopps

Would you rather LIVE in . . .

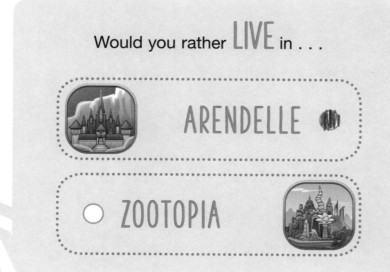

ARENDELLE

ZOOTOPIA

# Which Disney Princess Are You?

### ARE YOU BELLE OR ARIEL? RAPUNZEL OR MERIDA?

There have been important questions asked in the past, but this is the holy grail of all questions: Which Disney Princess is most like you? Your life will never be the same after this moment. And no, we're not exaggerating, but yes, you're welcome.

## QUESTION 1:

## MY FAVORITE WEEKEND ACTIVITY IS...

- ○ a. Curling up with a book
- ○ b. Exploring a farmers market
- ○ c. Cooking
- ◐ d. Going to a party
- ◑ e. Being outside

- ○ f. Dancing
- ◐ g. Having alone time
- ○ h. Hanging with friends
- ◑ i. Spending time with family
- ◑ j. Walking in the woods
- ◑ k. Looking for treasure

QUESTION 2:

# THE ANIMAL LEADING MY (inevitable) ROYAL PARADE IS . . .

- *a.* **A HORSE**
- *b.* **A TIGER**
- *c.* **AN ALLIGATOR**
- *d.* **A FEW MICE**
- *e.* **A BEAR**
- *f.* **AN OWL**
- *g.* **A CHAMELEON**
- *h.* **A DEER**
- *i.* **A DRAGON**
- *j.* **A RACCOON**
- *k.* **A CRAB**

## THE MOST IMPORTANT QUALITY I LOOK FOR IN A PRINCE IS . . .

a. Thoughtfulness

b. Humor

c. Fun-loving nature

d. Charm

e. I don't need a prince

f. Dancing skills

g. Smolder

h. Kindness

i. Honor

j. Personality

k. Dreaminess

# MY FAVORITE PLACE/TIME TO BURST INTO SONG IS . . .

- ○ *a.* A FIELD OF FLOWERS
- ○ *b.* MY GARDEN
- ○ *c.* ON THE GO
- ◍ *d.* WHILE DOING CHORES
- ○ *e.* I DON'T SING
- ○ *f.* A FOREST
- ○ *g.* EVERYWHERE

- ◍ *h.* WHILE I DAYDREAM
- ◍ *i.* IN MY ROOM
- ○ *j.* UNDER A WILLOW TREE
- ◍ *k.* AT THE BEACH

# MY FAVORITE HAIRSTYLE IS . . .

a. Half up, half down

b. A ponytail

c. I don't have a favorite

d. Whatever is the easiest to do in the morning

e. Curly

f. Down with a headband

g. Long—really, really long

h. A stylish bob

i. A high bun

j. Sleek and super straight

k. Natural

# SOMEDAY I WANT TO BE . . .

- ○ *a.* **A WRITER**
- ○ *b.* **AN EXPLORER**
- ○ *c.* **A BUSINESS OWNER**
- ⊗ *d.* **A FASHION DESIGNER**
- ⊗ *e.* **AN OLYMPIC ATHLETE**
- ○ *f.* **AN ANIMAL RIGHTS ACTIVIST**
- ○ *g.* **AN ARTIST**
- ⊗ *h.* **A PASTRY CHEF**
- ○ *i.* **A GENERAL**
- ○ *j.* **AN ENVIRONMENTAL LAWYER**
- ⊗ *k.* **A SINGER**

**QUESTION 7:**

# IN ONE WORD, MY STYLE IS . . .

○ a. Comfortable

◍ b. Girly

○ c. Vintage

○ d. Classic

○ e. Practical

○ f. Timeless

○ g. Bohemian

○ h. Retro

○ i. I don't have a style

◍ j. Functional

◍ k. Colorful

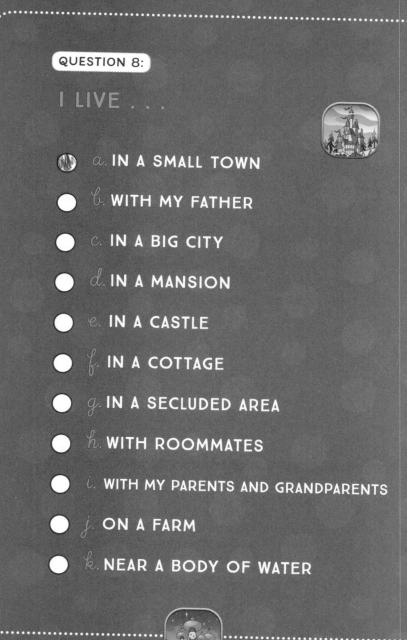

**QUESTION 8:**

## I LIVE . . .

- a. IN A SMALL TOWN
- b. WITH MY FATHER
- c. IN A BIG CITY
- d. IN A MANSION
- e. IN A CASTLE
- f. IN A COTTAGE
- g. IN A SECLUDED AREA
- h. WITH ROOMMATES
- i. WITH MY PARENTS AND GRANDPARENTS
- j. ON A FARM
- k. NEAR A BODY OF WATER

# IT'S 4 P.M.! THAT MEANS IT'S TIME TO . . .

- a. Have tea
- b. Take a walk
- c. Go to work
- d. Do my chores
- e. Go for a ride
- f. Take a nap
- g. Work on my chess game
- h. Have a snack
- i. Work out
- j. Spend time with friends
- k. Have band practice

# MY FAVORITE COLOR IS . . .

○ *a.* **YELLOW**

 *b.* **TURQUOISE**

○ *c.* **GREEN**

○ *d.* **WHITE**

○ *e.* **BROWN**

○ *f.* **PINK**

○ *g.* **PURPLE**

○ *h.* **RED**

○ *i.* **BLACK**

○ *j.* **ORANGE**

⊘ *k.* **BLUE**

FOR ANSWERS, TURN TO PAGES 98–101 OF THE ANSWER KEY.

# QUICK QUIZ!

NAME B.rooklyn

DATE

??  YOU'RE FEELING?

1. EVER BEEN SERIOUSLY **LOST**?

● No  ○ Yes, I

I have
I not ben Lost beco
to I stap closetomyfumily

2. **SHARKS** OR **TURTLES?**

○

3. HAVE YOU EVER DONE SOMETHING THAT YOU WERE **SCARED** OF DOING?

○ NO ● Yes, I Went on
a Bigrouicoster.

18

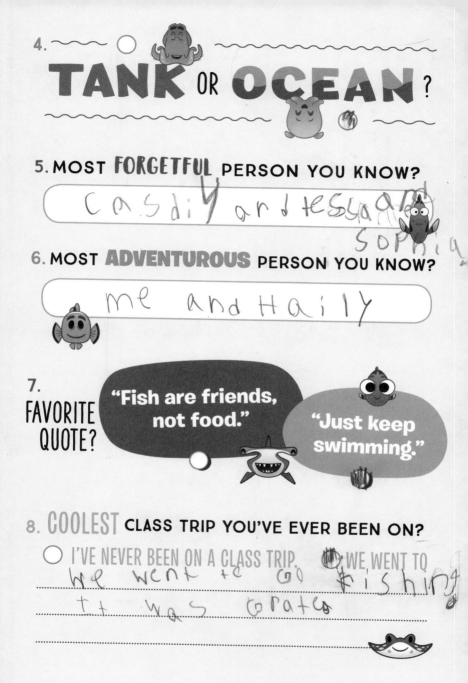

4.

# TANK OR OCEAN?

5. MOST **FORGETFUL** PERSON YOU KNOW?

Casdiy and tessa and
Sophia

6. MOST **ADVENTUROUS** PERSON YOU KNOW?

me and Haily

7. FAVORITE QUOTE?

"Fish are friends, not food."

"Just keep swimming."

8. **COOLEST** CLASS TRIP YOU'VE EVER BEEN ON?

○ I'VE NEVER BEEN ON A CLASS TRIP.   ● WE WENT TO

we went to go fishing
it was grates

# DISNEY PRINCE PLL

Looks like we've got a royal showdown! Which of your favorites will take the crown (and Disney prince superlative)? From best smile to best song to best date, it's up to you to determine the fate of these classic Disney heartthrobs.

## WHO HAS THE BEST EYES?

ALADDIN        ERIC        THE BEAST        NAVEEN

○                ○        ○

## WHO HAS THE BEST SMILE?

NAVEEN        FLYNN        ALADDIN        PRINCE CHARMING

○        ○        ○

## BEST **HAIR**?

JOHN
SMITH

THE
PRINCE
○

PRINCE
CHARMING
○

SHANG
○

## BEST **QUOTE**?

"Come, we
pucker!"

NAVEEN
○

"Here comes
the smolder."

FLYNN
○

"Um . . .
you—you fight
good."

SHANG

"I laugh in
the face of
danger."

SIMBA
○

"I'LL MAKE A MAN OUT OF YOU"

SHANG

"A WHOLE NEW WORLD"

ALADDIN

"ONCE UPON A DREAM"

PRINCE PHILLIP

"I JUST CAN'T WAIT TO BE KING"

SIMBA

# BEST DATE?

## ALADDIN'S MAGIC CARPET RIDE

○

The Beast's Enchanted Waltz

○

## NAVEEN'S BOAT DECK DINNER

○

## FLYNN'S LANTERN BOAT RIDE

○

Eric's Firefly Boat Ride

# BEST **HOUSE?**

PRINCE CHARMING

THE BEAST ◯

ERIC ◯

SIMBA ◯

FLYNN
+
MAXIMUS
○

ALADDIN
+
ABU
○

ERIC
+
MAX

PHILLIP
+
SAMSON
○

# HOW WELL DO YOU KNOW
## Alice in Wonderland?

This quiz gets curiouser and curiouser. Try your hand at this *Alice in Wonderland* trivia.

## What is the name of Alice's cat?

- a. Lucy
- b. Molly
- c. Missy
- d. Dinah

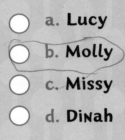

## What does the "Drink Me" potion NOT taste like?

- a. Cherry tart
- b. Pineapple
- c. Mashed potatoes
- d. Roast turkey

26

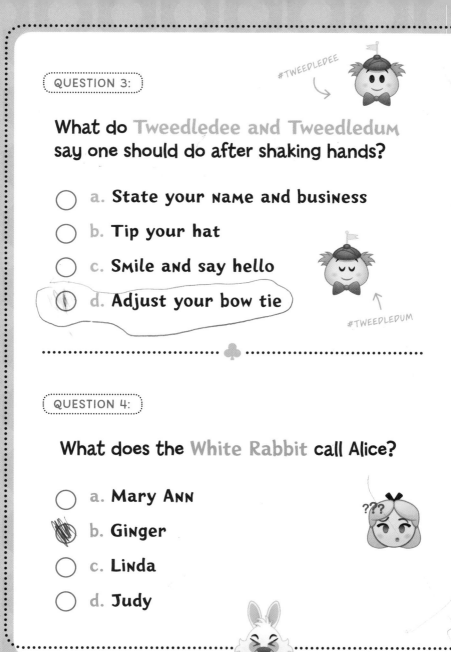

#TWEEDLEDEE

**What do** Tweedledee and Tweedledum **say one should do after shaking hands?**

○ a. State your name and business

○ b. Tip your hat

○ c. Smile and say hello

○ d. Adjust your bow tie

#TWEEDLEDUM

♣

**What does the** White Rabbit **call Alice?**

○ a. Mary Ann

○ b. Ginger

○ c. Linda

○ d. Judy

## How slow is the White Rabbit's watch?

○ a. One hour

○ b. One day

○ c. Two days

● d. A week

#HESLATE

## What is the name of the lizard with a ladder?

○ a. Paul

● b. Danny

○ c. Lou

○ d. Bill

**QUESTION 7:**

## What card suit is on the White Rabbit's shirt?

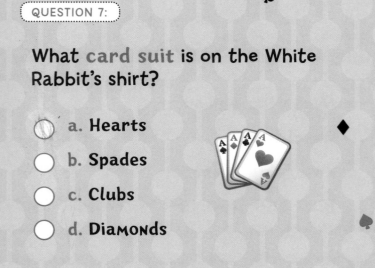

- ○ a. Hearts
- ○ b. Spades
- ○ c. Clubs
- ○ d. Diamonds

**QUESTION 8:**

## What song do the flowers sing to Alice?

- ○ a. "Golden Afternoon"
- ○ b. "Lovely Lily of the Valley"
- ○ c. "Tell It to the Tulips"
- ○ d. "Blame It on the Begonias"

**What advice does the Caterpillar give to Alice?**

○ a. Mind your manners

○ b. Watch out

○ c. Keep your temper

○ d. Look both ways before crossing the street

♣

**What occasion are the Mad Hatter and the March Hare celebrating?**

○ a. A birthday

○ b. An unbirthday

○ c. The Queen's birthday

○ d. Teatime

#CHEERS!

**QUESTION 11:**

## What number is written on the card on the Mad Hatter's hat?

○ a. **10/6**

○ b. **14**

○ c. **6/10**

○ d. **1/4**

♣

**QUESTION 12:**

## What animal does the Queen use for a croquet mallet?

○ a. **Penguin**

○ b. **Flamingo**

○ c. **Giraffe**

○ d. **Lizard**

# DYNAMIC DISNEY DUOS:
## Complete Their **CONVERSATIONS!**

Like birds of a feather, these Disney characters stick together.
Actually, they talk together. Or argue. Sometimes they sing.
And some characters know each other so well they can speak in
unison. See how well you can remember the conversations of
Disney's dynamic (and talkative) duos.

**1.**

"Couldn't keep quiet, could we? Just had to
invite him to stay, didn't we? Serve him tea. Sit
in the master's chair. Pet the ___ ___ ___ ___ ___!"

"I was trying to be

_____."

**2.**

"Flounder, don't be such a ___ Guppy."

"I'm not a ___ Guppy."

**3.**

"I can't take it anymore! If I gotta choke down on one more of those moldy, _c r a c k e r s_ crackers . . . BAM! Whack!"

"_____ _____, Iago."

**4.**

"You are a child's plaything!"

"You are a _____, _____ little man, and you have my pity."

"It's long-term memory. You'll get  _____ in there."

 "C'MON! Think positive!"

"I act scary, Mike. But most of the time, I'm _____."

 "How come you never told me that before?"

"Because we weren't _____ before."

7.

"You came back."

"Nobody gets _____

_____."

8.

"COME ON, trust ME ON this ONE."

"Trust you?"

"Yes, trust. _____  _____

_____  ____."

**9.**

"Oh, gee. I always thought they were balls of gas burNiNg billioNs of Miles away."

"Pumbaa, with you,

_____

_____."

**10.**

"Well, angelfish, the solution to your problem is simple. The only way to get what you want is to _____

__ _____ yourself."

"CaN you do that?"

"My dear, sweet child. That's what I do. It's what I live for—to help unfortunate merfolk like yourself,

_____ _____ with no one else

to turn to."

**11.**

"You know, waitress, I finally figured out what's wrong with you."

"Have you, now?"

"You do not know how to _____ _____."

**12.**

"No! I don't trust your _____!"

"Excuse me?"

"Who marries a man they just met?"

"It's _____    _____!"

# WOULD **you** RATHER

## SCENARIOS

Rev your engines for an especially silly, entirely wacky round of Would You Rather, Disney•Pixar-style. Whether you choose to take a walk in someone else's boots, dabble in whale speak, or take a ride on the *Axiom*, the world of Disney•Pixar is your oyster. Grab your friends, and go have an adventure.

○   ○   ○

Would you rather have one
**GIANT EYEBALL** or **BLUE**-and-**PURPLE** fur?

Would you rather travel by A HOUSE FLOATING ON BALLOONS or by the AXIOM?

House with Balloons

Would you rather have **Remy** control your every movement, or have to pretend to **be inanimate** around humans?

Would you rather have a **talking dog** or a **talking dinosaur**?

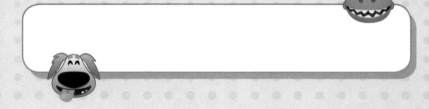

Would you rather have **SUPER STRENGTH** or SUPER *SPEED*?

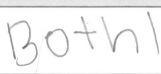

Both!

Would you rather learn **ARCHERY** from Merida
or **RACING** from Lightning McQueen?

Merida

Would you rather live on the
**GREAT BARRIER REEF** or in the **PARR HOME**?

Parr home

Would you rather be able to
**speak to whales**, or live in a world
of **anthropomorphic cars**?

Would you rather smell like *cotton candy* or *strawberries*?

Would you rather live with **Kari** the babysitter or **M-O**?

Would you rather have DORY'S MEMORY or ANGER'S TEMPER?

Who would you rather invite to your next birthday party, **RANDALL** or **BRUCE**?

Don't you just love Disney dads? Who doesn't? Now it's time to figure out who said what. Get ready, get set, and go!

1. "WELL, WHAT ARE WE WAITING FOR? I'LL HAVE THIS THING FIXED IN NO TIME!"

2. "YOU KNOW, MOONING ABOUT, DAYDREAMING, SINGING TO HERSELF. YOU HAVEN'T NOTICED, HMMM?"

3. "SO WHENEVER YOU FEEL ALONE, JUST REMEMBER THAT THOSE KINGS WILL ALWAYS BE THERE TO GUIDE YOU."

4. "WAIT A MINUTE, YOU ALREADY TOLD ME WHICH WAY THE BOAT WENT."

5. "FOR A TRUE HERO ISN'T MEASURED BY THE SIZE OF HIS STRENGTH, BUT BY THE STRENGTH OF HIS HEART."

6. "MY, WHAT BEAUTIFUL BLOSSOMS WE HAVE THIS YEAR. BUT LOOK, THIS ONE'S LATE. BUT I'LL BET THAT WHEN IT BLOOMS, IT WILL BE THE MOST BEAUTIFUL OF ALL."

7. "PEOPLE KEEP COMING UP WITH NEW WAYS TO CELEBRATE MEDIOCRITY, BUT IF SOMEONE IS GENUINELY EXCEPTIONAL . . ."

8. "SOMETIMES OUR PATHS ARE CHOSEN FOR US."

9. "YOU'VE CERTAINLY PROVEN YOUR WORTH AS FAR AS I'M CONCERNED. IT'S THAT LAW THAT'S THE PROBLEM."

10. "WHO WOULD WANT TO GO ANYWHERE ELSE?"

FOR ANSWERS, TURN TO PAGE 103 OF THE ANSWER KEY.

# QUICK QUIZ!

**NAME** Brooklyn

**DATE** 1-29-20

**YOU'RE FEELING?**

1. **HOW MANY SIBLINGS DO YOU HAVE?**

   ○ None  ● I have _I have_
   _2_

2. **SUMMER OR WINTER?**

   _Both_

3. **FAVORITE WINTER SPORT?**

   Skiing

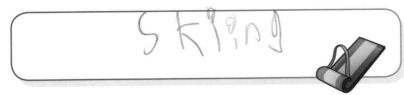

4. **CRAZIEST THING YOU'VE EVER DONE?**

*Siing the psp song!*

5. **PERSON YOU KNOW WHO'S MOST LIKELY TO** *fall in love too easily*?

*Conner, Jackson, John.*

6. **FAVORITE QUOTE**

"Some people are worth melting for."

"Only an act of true love can thaw a frozen heart."

7. **NAME SOMETHING THAT YOU NEED TO LET GO OF AND WHY:** *Grace, she is mean to me.*

8. **HOW DO YOU REACT WHEN YOU'RE ANGRY?**

# MATCH THE *Disney Princess*
## NAME TO ITS MEANING!

Much like iconic musicians, Disney Princesses have become synonymous with their first names. Being able to name them all is one thing, but can you identify the meaning behind each Disney Princess name?

(Some Disney Princess names have several meanings, but we decided to make things easier by attaching a single definition to each name. Don't worry—we won't try to trick you by including multiple correct meanings as answers.)

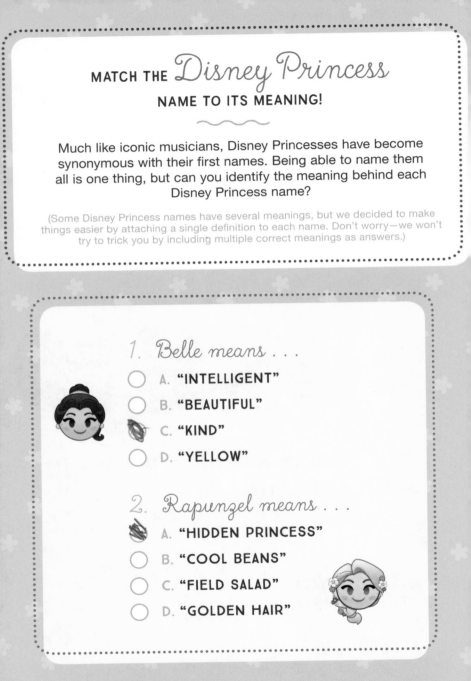

*1. Belle means . . .*

- A. **"INTELLIGENT"**
- B. **"BEAUTIFUL"**
- C. **"KIND"**
- D. **"YELLOW"**

*2. Rapunzel means . . .*

- A. **"HIDDEN PRINCESS"**
- B. **"COOL BEANS"**
- C. **"FIELD SALAD"**
- D. **"GOLDEN HAIR"**

3. *Tiana means . . .*

- ○ A. **"SUCCESS"**
- ⊘ B. **"TRUE"**
- ○ C. **"BEIGNET"**
- ○ D. **"LIGHT"**

4. *Cinderella means . . .*

- ⊘ A. **"DUTIFUL CHILD"**
- ○ B. **"LITTLE ASHES"**
- ○ C. **"SHOELESS MAIDEN"**
- ○ D. **"DUST COLLECTOR"**

5. *Mulan means . . .*

- ○ A. **"WOOD ORCHID"**
- ⊘ B. **"ADVERSITY BLOSSOM"**
- ○ C. **"UNIQUE LOTUS"**
- ○ D. **"UNCOMMON ROSE"**

### 6. Aurora means . . .

A. "DREAM"

B. "TIRED"

C. "ASLEEP"

D. "DAWN"

### 7. Ariel means . . .

A. "WATER"

B. "PASSENGER"

C. "LIONESS"

D. "SWIMMER"

### 8. Jasmine is . . .

A. A TYPE OF FLOWER

B. A SPECIES OF TIGER

C. A SPECIES OF BIRD

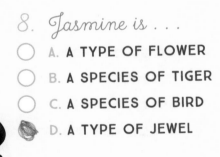

D. A TYPE OF JEWEL

## 9. Pocahontas means . . .

- A. "PEACEFUL ONE"
- B. "FEARLESS DAUGHTER" ~~✗~~
- C. "INSIGHTFUL WARRIOR"
- D. "PLAYFUL ONE"

## 10. Snow White's name . . .

- A. REFERS TO HER COMPLEXION
- B. REFERS TO HER FAVORITE SEASON
- C. REFERS TO HER BODY TEMPERATURE
- D. REFERS TO HER PERSONALITY

## 11. Merida means . . .

- A. "A WOMAN WHO LOVES BEARS"
- B. "A WOMAN WHO HAS ACHIEVED A PLACE OF HONOR"
- C. "A WOMAN WHO IS A SKILLED ARCHER"
- D. "A WOMAN WHO IS WISE BEYOND HER YEARS"

FOR ANSWERS, TURN TO PAGE 104 OF THE ANSWER KEY.

# THE **HARDEST**
## DISNEY•PIXAR QUIZ **EVER!**

Think you're a Disney•Pixar movie expert? Good!
This quiz was made especially for you!

 1. What is the name of **Merida's horse** in *Brave*?

- A. **ANGUS**
- B. **HAMISH**
- C. **GORDON**
- D. **FERGUS**

 2. **True** or **false:** *Toy Story* was released in 1996.

- **TRUE**
- **FALSE**

3. What Disney·Pixar movie is this quote from? **"I saw a really hairy guy; he looked like a bear."**

A. *UP*

B. *THE INCREDIBLES*

C. *INSIDE OUT*

D. *BRAVE*

4. In the movie *Cars*, what **color** is **Sally Carrera**?

A. SILVER

B. BLUE

C. PURPLE

D. GREEN

5. In *Ratatouille*, what is the **name of the restaurant** Colette, Linguini, and Remy open at the end of the movie?

A. CAFÉ DE RATATOUILLE

B. CAFÉ DE REMY

C. REMY'S

D. LA RATATOUILLE

6. **Finish the quote:** "Well, you can't never let anything happen to him. Then nothing would ever happen to him. Not much fun for little _____." **Dory** (*Finding Nemo*)

○ A. HARPO

○ B. NEMO

○ C. FABIO

○ D. ELMO

7. Who **composed** the music for *Monsters, Inc.*?

○ A. DANNY ELFMAN

○ B. ALAN MENKEN

○ C. HOWARD ASHMAN

○ D. RANDY NEWMAN

8. What does **Edna Mode** believe looking back distracts from?

○ A. THE FUTURE

○ B. THE NOW

○ C. SUCCESS

○ D. HAPPINESS

9. **Finish the quote:** "Good work, men. _____ blocks down and only _____ more to go." **Buzz Lightyear** (*Toy Story 2*)

- ○ A. EIGHT, TWO
- ○ B. FIVE, FOUR
- ○ C. THREE, SEVENTEEN
- ○ D. TWO, NINETEEN

10. **True** or **false:** Hayden Panettiere voiced **Dot** in *A Bug's Life*.

- ○ TRUE
- ○ FALSE

11. **Who said this quote?** "Maybe. But when you lose, no one will let you forget it."

- ○ A. BOB PARR
- ○ B. BUZZ LIGHTYEAR
- ○ C. ANGER
- ○ D. MIKE WAZOWSKI

# CAN YOU
# UNSCRAMBLE
## THE DISNEY VILLAINS' SIDEKICKS' NAMES?

Disney Villains are great, but sometimes it's their furry, feathery, slimy, and/or scaly sidekicks that put them over the top as some of our favorite characters. While you may know some of the sidekicks' famous quotes, scenes, or plots, can you unscramble their names?

## IPNA AND AIPCN

1.

## OGIA

2.

## SMAOTFL AND MJATSE

3.

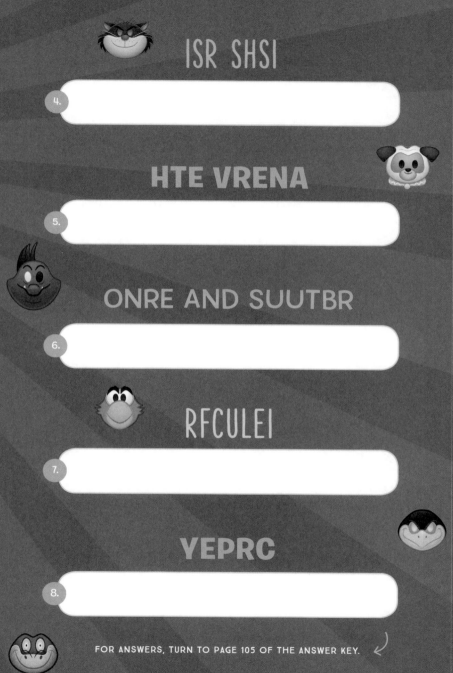

ISR SHSI

4.

HTE VRENA

5.

ONRE AND SUUTBR

6.

RFCULEI

7.

YEPRC

8.

FOR ANSWERS, TURN TO PAGE 105 OF THE ANSWER KEY.

# CAN YOU GUESS THE DISNEY CHARACTER AND MOVIE
# FROM THE TWEET?

Have you ever wondered what it would be like if Disney characters could tweet about their epic adventures? We have! Can you guess what character/movie each tweet is from?

**1.** Just a casual Friday night soaring through the sky. **#magiccarpetride**

CHARACTER

MOVIE

**#iwantmore**

**2.** TFW you're just really done with water.

CHARACTER

MOVIE

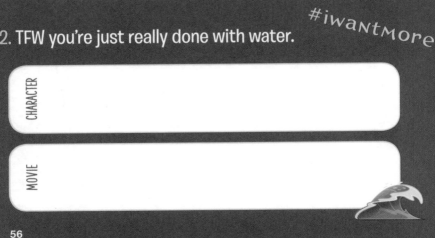

## 3. Tweeting for the first time in forever!  #lol

CHARACTER

MOVIE

## 4. ICYMI: I'm awake!  #BESTALARMCLOCKEVER

CHARACTER

MOVIE

## 5. Remember when I played croquet with a flamingo?  #tbt

CHARACTER

MOVIE

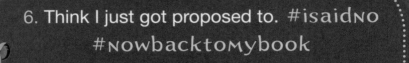

6. Think I just got proposed to. #isaidno
#nowbacktomybook

CHARACTER

MOVIE

7. TBH I'm never going back there.

#noworries

CHARACTER

MOVIE

8. On a train headed to the big city! #ahhhhh
#reportingforduty

CHARACTER

MOVIE

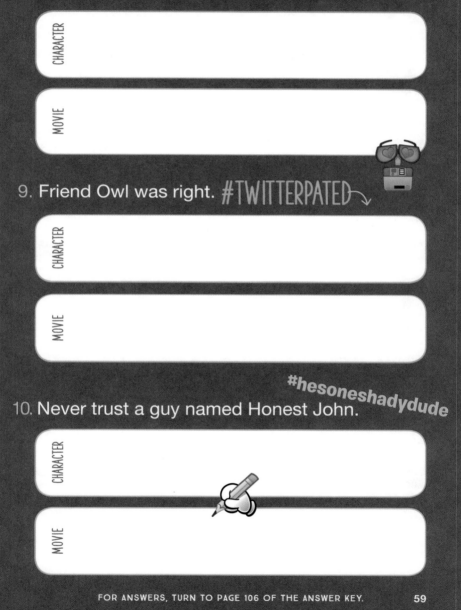

9. Friend Owl was right. #TWITTERPATED

CHARACTER

MOVIE

#hesoneshadydude

10. Never trust a guy named Honest John.

CHARACTER

MOVIE

FOR ANSWERS, TURN TO PAGE 106 OF THE ANSWER KEY.

# Come up with **ten of your own**
Disney character tweets and **#hashtags**
based on the emoji!

#

#

#

#

#

# 

........................................................................

........................................................................

# ........................................................................

........................................................................

........................................................................

# ........................................................................

........................................................................

........................................................................

# ........................................................................

........................................................................

........................................................................

# ........................................................................

........................................................................

........................................................................

# ........................................................................

# EIGHT TIMES YOU WERE WATCHING A DISNEY•PIXAR MOVIE AND SAID,

## "IT'S ME."

Remy may be a rat with otherworldly cooking and human-control skills, and Mike may be a one-eyed monster with a knack for telling jokes, but let's face it: you've come to realize that you are more like these Disney•Pixar characters than you are like other actual humans. Here are all the times you might've said "It's me" while watching a Disney•Pixar movie.

**1.** When **Edna Mode** threw all this shade at Bob with just her eyeballs. (This **handy look** is very useful for all the times you've heard and/or seen something and thought, *Absolutely not.*)

2. When WALL•E was single and ready to robo-mingle. (*Small! Dark! Handsome!* This rusty dreamboat is every hopeless romantic's spirit robot.)

3. Any time GERALD did literally anything. (Socially awkward? *Check.* Generally oblivious? *Check.* Constantly wanting to chill on the cool kids' rock all day? *Check.* Gerald is everyone.) (*P.S. We are obsessed with Gerald.*)

EXHIBIT A.

EXHIBIT B.

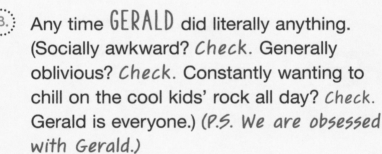

**4.** When Remy was in CHEESE HEAVEN. (Whether your cheese style is cheddar, gouda, mozzarella, sliced, grated, shredded, or stringed, you know this face.)

**5.** When *LIGHTNING MCQUEEN* was a precision instrument of *speed* and *aerodynamics* (a.k.a. how you look when the last bell rings).

**6.** When **Fear** had a major panic attack over being called on in class. (Because all you want to do when you're the new kid is be forced to stand up in front of the whole class and say words.)

7. When **ANDY'S TOY SQUAD** was part of a really cute growing-up montage. (Andy's childhood is such an integral part of your childhood that you have trouble distinguishing the two. For example, you wrote *ANDY* on your favorite toy's foot, and your name is definitely not *ANDY*.)

8. Speaking of montages, when *Carl* and *Ellie* were ultimate *#couplegoals*. (So this one might be less of an "It's me" and more of an *"I really, really, really, really want this to be me one day."*)

*#couplegoals*

What **Disney•Pixar** movie moment made you say **"It's me"**? Grab a friend and list your eight answers below.

1.

2.

3.

4.

5.

6.

7.

8.

# ARE YOU THE Ultimate
# Disney Villain FAN?

So you think you're the biggest Disney Villain fan out there? In true villainous fashion, we're here to challenge you on that! We harnessed our inner Disney Villains and came up with this sinister quiz meant to stump even the most die-hard aficionado. Let's see how you do!

1. In *Pinocchio*, what's **Honest John's** full name?

   - A. JONATHAN FOULFELLOW WORTHMAN
   - B. JOHN WORTHINGTON FOULFELLOW
   - C. JOHN WITHERMAN FIENDFELLOW
   - D. JONATHAN WORTHINGTON FIENDFELLOW

2. When Jafar turns into a cobra, what **color** are the stripes on his skin?

   - A. RED **AND BLACK**
   - B. YELLOW **AND RED**
   - C. GREEN **AND BLACK**
   - D. BLACK AND GOLD

3. In *The Lion King*, Scar says that Mufasa got the brute strength in the family. What did **Scar** get?

   - A. LOOKS
   - B. TALENT
   - C. CHARISMA
   - D. BRAINS

4. Who voiced **Ursula** in *The Little Mermaid?*

   ○ A. ELEANOR AUDLEY
   ○ B. PAT CARROLL
   ○ C. LUCILLE LA VERNE
   ○ D. VERNA FELTON

5. In *101 Dalmatians,* how did **Cruella** and **Anita** first know each other?

   ○ A. THEY WERE NEIGHBORS
   ○ B. THEY WENT TO SCHOOL TOGETHER
   ○ C. THEY WERE COWORKERS
   ○ D. THEY'RE SISTERS

6. What is the name of **Captain Hook's ship?**

   ○ A. *THE HAPPY DODGER*
   ○ B. *THE JOLLY ROGER*
   ○ C. *THE ANGRY DODGER*
   ○ D. *THE FLYING ROGER*

7. In the song **"Gaston,"** the crowd sings "Give _____ hurrahs!"

   ○ A. FIVE
   ○ B. TWELVE
   ○ C. THREE
   ○ D. EIGHT

#WHENIWASALAD

8. What kind of **magical being** is Maleficent in *Sleeping Beauty*?

- ○ A. **WITCH**
- ○ B. **FAIRY**
- ○ C. **GOBLIN**
- ○ D. **MERMAID**

9. In *Robin Hood*, what **symbol** can be seen on the back of Prince John's handheld mirror?

- ○ A. **A TULIP**
- ○ B. **A FLEUR-DE-LIS**
- ○ C. **A SWORD**
- ○ D. **COINS**

10. When the **Evil Queen** in *Snow White and the Seven Dwarfs* disguises herself as an old hag, what color are her **eyes**?

- ○ A. **GREEN**
- ○ B. **BLUE**
- ○ C. **BROWN**
- ○ D. **PURPLE**

11. How did **Mother Gothel** break out of the castle when she stole Rapunzel as a baby?

- ○ A. **THROUGH THE FRONT DOOR**
- ○ B. **BY VANISHING INTO THIN AIR**
- ○ C. **THROUGH AN OPEN WINDOW**
- ○ D. **BY JUMPING OFF THE ROOF**

12. What **color** is Lady Tremaine's **sleeping cap** in the animated *Cinderella*?

    ○ A. PINK
    ○ B. BLUE
    ○ C. GRAY
    ○ D. PURPLE

13. In *Wreck-It Ralph*, what was **King Candy's** character's name?

    ○ A. TURBO
    ○ B. SPEED
    ○ C. LIGHTNING
    ○ D. ROCKET

14. Which of these things does the Queen of Hearts **not ask** Alice to do when they first meet?

    ○ A. LOOK UP
    ○ B. CURTSY
    ○ C. TURN OUT HER TOES
    ○ D. APPLAUD

15. What **color** are Governor Ratcliffe's **hair bows** in *Pocahontas*?

    ○ A. BLUE
    ○ B. ORANGE
    ○ C. GREEN
    ○ D. RED

16. In *Hercules*, Zeus and Hades are brothers. Who's **younger**?

- ○ A. HADES
- ○ B. ZEUS

17. When Kronk pulls the wrong lever in *The Emperor's New Groove*, what **animal** does Yzma pull out of the water with her?

- ○ A. CROCODILE
- ○ B. WHALE
- ○ C. FROG
- ○ D. HIPPO

18. What is the name of Ursula's **human** alter ego?

- ○ A. JESSICA
- ○ B. MARISSA
- ○ C. ELIZABETH
- ○ D. VANESSA

19. Eleanor Audley voiced which **two** Disney Villains?

- ○ A. MALEFICENT AND LADY TREMAINE
- ○ B. URSULA AND MALEFICENT
- ○ C. CRUELLA DE VIL AND MALEFICENT
- ○ D. LADY TREMAINE AND URSULA

20. What are the names of Cruella De Vil's **henchmen**?

- ○ A. EDGAR AND WALLACE
- ○ B. HORACE AND JASPER
- ○ C. MIKE AND PETER
- ○ D. HOWARD AND RAYMOND

21. In *The Hunchback of Notre Dame*, **how many rings** does Claude Frollo wear in total?

○ A. TWO
○ B. ONE
○ C. THREE
○ D. FOUR

22. Which of Captain Hook's **hands** has a hook on it?

○ A. LEFT
○ B. RIGHT

23. What does Gaston tell Belle is "more important than books"?

○ A. LOOKS
○ B. EGGS
○ C. STRENGTH
○ D. HIMSELF

24. What is Jafar's **title** at the beginning of *Aladdin*?

○ A. ROYAL VIZIER
○ B. HAND OF THE SULTAN
○ C. SULTAN
○ D. SHAH OF AGRABAH

25. In *The Jungle Book*, what kind of **snake** is Kaa?

○ A. COBRA
○ B. PYTHON
○ C. ANACONDA
○ D. BOA

#HISSSSS

FOR ANSWERS, TURN TO PAGES 106–107 OF THE ANSWER KEY.

1. WHEN YOU'RE IN A **MOOD**, YOU . . .

   ○ CURSE A BABY  ○ STORM A CASTLE
   ○ POISON AN APPLE

2. IF YOU WERE A DISNEY Villain, WHAT WOULD YOUR superpower BE AND WHY?

3. WHO WOULD YOUR sidekick BE?

4. **PURPLE** OR **GREEN?**

5. **WHEN YOU** *accidentally* **HIT THE FRONT-FACING CAMERA, YOU LOOK . . .**

*beastly*

*perfect*

*confused*

6.

"You poor, simple fools, thinking you could defeat me. Me, the mistress of all evil!"

What would your **EVIL QUOTE** be?

7. **THE MOST** *evil thing* **YOU'VE DONE IS . . .**

8. **YOUR EVIL LAIR WOULD BE IN A . . .**

# GUESS THE DISNEY MOVIE BASED ON THE EMOJIS!

It's a proven fact: Disney fans 💜 emojis. Why else would we use these adorable little tech treasures to express our excitement and make tributes to our favorite Disney films? Is your emoji-decoding game at 100 percent 🐰 or are you as clueless as Goofy? 🐶 Don your (great mouse) detective cap and put your deciphering skills to the test to see if you can name the movie from just a series of emojis.

1.

2.

3.

4.

5.

6.

7.

8.

9.

10.

FOR ANSWERS, TURN TO PAGE 108 OF THE ANSWER KEY.

# UNSCRAMBLE
## THE DISNEY ANAGRAMS

Who doesn't love a good Disney quote? See if you can unscramble these anagrams to guess the Disney quote, and then match each quote to its speaker!

### THE CUBE TO THE THUD

1.

### THREATEN DEVIOUS TRUE

2.

### YOU TO A YEAR

3.

### IM SWEET KING JUMPS

4.

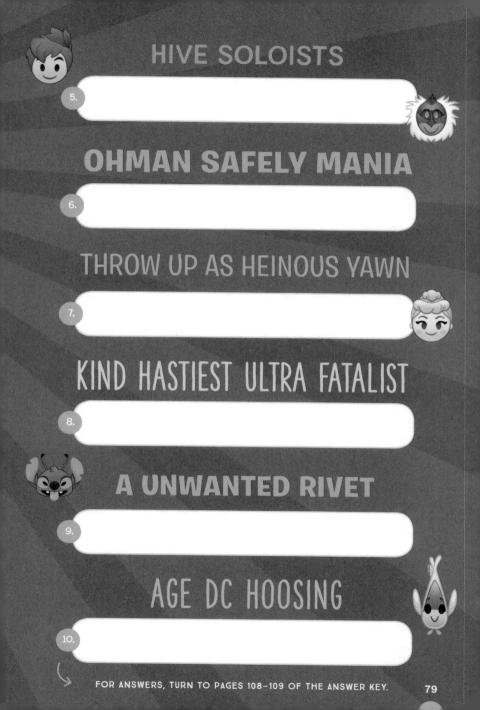

# HIVE SOLOISTS

5.

# OHMAN SAFELY MANIA

6.

# THROW UP AS HEINOUS YAWN

7.

# KIND HASTIEST ULTRA FATALIST

8.

# A UNWANTED RIVET

9.

# AGE DC HOOSING

10.

FOR ANSWERS, TURN TO PAGES 108–109 OF THE ANSWER KEY.

# WHICH *Disney Date* SHOULD YOU GO ON BASED ON YOUR *Astrological* SIGN?

Whether you've been with your sweetheart for years or just started dating someone, we all could use some date-night inspiration. And perhaps that inspiration could come from Disney movies! (In fact, we think it can.) We got an expert to align each zodiac sign with the perfect Disney date for you and your special someone.

*Let's find out what it is!*

## *Aquarius* January 20–February 18

### YOU SHOULD GO ON
### *Tiana and Naveen's* DATE!

You are sweet, imaginative, and always original. So, like Naveen, you can plan a river cruise dinner for your sweetheart. Or maybe you can cook dinner for your sweetie and watch *The Princess and the Frog*. Perfect date night!

## Pisces February 19–March 20

### YOU SHOULD GO ON A ROMANTIC BOAT RIDE LIKE *Eric and Ariel*!

Your compassionate, natural, and intuitive spirit makes a quiet romantic boat ride the perfect date for you. The background music ("Kiss the Girl") is also perfect for the music-loving Pisces.

## Aries March 21–April 19

### YOU SHOULD GO DANCING LIKE *Cinderella and Prince Charming*!

You love to move, so a night full of dancing is the perfect date for you! Just make sure you are home before the clock strikes twelve, and keep your shoes on!

## Taurus April 20–May 20

### YOU SHOULD GO ON A WALK THROUGH THE PARK LIKE *Pongo and Perdita*!

Like Pongo, you're patient but practical. He wasn't going to wait for the right moment to meet his true love, and he didn't hold back. A lovely stroll through the park followed by afternoon tea is ideal for your Disney-inspired date.

## *Gemini* May 21–June 20

### YOU SHOULD GO ON *WALL•E and EVE'S* STAR-DANCING DATE!

You're curious and gentle like WALL•E. So the perfect date for you includes watching a movie, followed by putting on some classic tunes like Louis Armstrong's "La Vie en Rose" and dancing under the stars.

## *Cancer* June 21–July 22

### YOU SHOULD GO ON *Flynn and Rapunzel's* LANTERN BOAT-RIDE DATE!

You're full of imagination, loyalty, and generosity. So get crafty and turn your yard into a whimsical date, with lanterns and some music to re-create this romantic moment.

## *Leo*  July 23–August 22

### YOU SHOULD GO ON *Belle and the Beast's* BREAKFAST DATE!

You may have a temper at times, but you are warmhearted and generous. Re-create their breakfast date, go outside and enjoy nature, and finish the date by reading together. (And if you can give someone a whole library like the Beast did, you totally should.)

## *Virgo*  August 23–September 22

### YOU SHOULD GO ON *Lady and Tramp's* SPAGHETTI DINNER DATE!

You are loyal, kind, and practical. So a classic romantic dinner is just right for you. It's simple and timeless. And you may even share a plate (or at least some pasta) with your sweetheart.

## Libra    September 23–October 22

### YOU SHOULD GO ON *Aladdin and Jasmine's* MAGIC CARPET RIDE!

You are kind and a lover of peace and harmony, so this magical date is for you. You may not have a magic carpet on hand to travel around the entire world, but you can book a weekend getaway! Pack your bags!

---

## Scorpio    October 23–November 21

### YOU SHOULD GO ON *Pocahontas and John Smith's* HIKING DATE!

You are resourceful, passionate, and brave, so a hiking date is perfect for you. Pocahontas and John Smith do all sorts of outdoor activities, and so should you and your sweetheart! Enjoy all the voices of the mountains and good company.

## Sagittarius  November 22–December 21

### YOU SHOULD GO ON *Nala and Simba's* STARGAZING DATE!

You are spontaneous and free-spirited, so this spur-of-the-moment date is for you. Grab your sweetheart and spend the night gazing at the beautiful stars above!

## Capricorn  December 22–January 19

### YOU SHOULD GO ON *Ellie and Carl's* PICNIC!

You like a date that's all planned out and no-stress, like Ellie and Carl's picnic. So pack your picnic basket and a blanket and enjoy a nice day outside. Capricorns are hard workers, so it would be good to take a break, look at some clouds, and daydream.

# CAN YOU GUESS THE DISNEY MOVIE BASED ON THE
# TAGLINE?

Every great story has a meaningful message, and the best ones can be boiled down to just a couple of words. If you've seen a few Disney trailers and posters in your day, it's time to put your memory to the test.

1. **"The most beautiful love story ever told."**
   - ○ A. *POCAHONTAS*
   - ○ B. *SLEEPING BEAUTY*
   - ○ C. *BEAUTY AND THE BEAST*
   - ○ D. *THE LITTLE MERMAID*

2. **"The greatest adventure of all is finding our place in the Circle of Life."**
   - ○ A. *THE LION KING*
   - ○ B. *A BUG'S LIFE*
   - ○ C. *THE JUNGLE BOOK*
   - ○ D. *THE LION KING II*

3. **"There's one in every family."**
   - ○ A. *MARY POPPINS*
   - ○ B. *A GOOFY MOVIE*
   - ○ C. *CHICKEN LITTLE*
   - ○ D. *LILO & STITCH*

4. **"It's all about . . . me!"**
   - ○ A. *A BUG'S LIFE*
   - ○ B. *HERCULES*
   - ○ C. *ALADDIN*
   - ○ D. *THE EMPEROR'S NEW GROOVE*

**5.** "Midnight never strikes when you're in love."
- ○ A. *ALICE IN WONDERLAND*
- ○ B. *BEAUTY AND THE BEAST*
- ○ C. *CINDERELLA*
- ○ D. *LADY AND THE TRAMP*

**6.** "They're taking adventures to new lengths."
- ○ A. *THE RESCUERS*
- ○ B. *TANGLED*
- ○ C. *ALADDIN*
- ○ D. *THE BLACK CAULDRON*

**7.** "Welcome to the urban jungle."
- ○ A. *ZOOTOPIA*
- ○ B. *THE PRINCESS AND THE FROG*
- ○ C. *THE ARISTOCATS*
- ○ D. *THE JUNGLE BOOK*

**8.** "An American legend come to life."
- ○ A. *THE PRINCESS AND THE FROG*
- ○ B. *BAMBI*
- ○ C. *HOME ON THE RANGE*
- ○ D. *POCAHONTAS*

**9.** "Find your place in the universe."
- ○ A. *WALL•E*
- ○ B. *TREASURE PLANET*
- ○ C. *BIG HERO 6*
- ○ D. *THE NIGHTMARE BEFORE CHRISTMAS*

**10.** "The ocean is calling."
- ○ A. *MOANA*
- ○ B. *TREASURE PLANET*
- ○ C. *FINDING NEMO*
- ○ D. *LILO & STITCH*

FOR ANSWERS, TURN TO PAGE 109 OF THE ANSWER KEY.

# QUICK QUIZ!

NAME

DATE

??? YOU'RE FEELING?

○ ○ ○ ○

1. **BOOKS** OR **LOOKS?**

○ ○

2. FAVORITE QUOTE

"Cheer up, child. It'll turn out all right in the end. You'll see."

○

"If it's not Baroque, don't fix it."

○

3. DESCRIBE YOURSELF IN **THREE WORDS**:

1. ........................................................................

2. ........................................................................

3. ........................................................................

## 4. WOULD YOU RATHER . . .

FIGHT A GROUP OF ANGRY VILLAGERS ○

FIGHT OFF HUNGRY WOLVES ○

## 5. WHAT IS YOUR *favorite book* TO GET LOST IN?

#Somethingtherethatwasnttherebefore

## 6. WHAT'S THE BETTER #HASHTAG? →

#beastmakeover

## 7. ○ HOW I THINK I SING

HOW I ACTUALLY SING ○

## 8. BELLE WANTS *adventure* IN THE GREAT, WIDE SOMEWHERE. WHERE *do you want to go* ON AN ADVENTURE?

# MATCH THE EMOJI TO THE OVERLY DRAMATIC TITLE

Below are ten overly dramatic titles to Disney movies. Name each movie and then match it to the emoji pairings on the opposite page!

1. Diamond in the Rough ....................................

2. Betrayal in the Pride Lands ....................................

3. The Last Petal ....................................

4. The Flower That Blooms ....................................

5. Chasing Floating Lanterns ....................................

6. When Ice Meets the Heart ....................................

7. A Tale of Land and Sea ....................................

8. A Hero's Journey ....................................

9. The Longest Sleep ....................................

10. Painting Roses Red ....................................

# MATCH THE WORD PAIR TO THE DISNEY CHARACTER!

There are countless words that can be used to describe our favorite Disney characters. Don't even get us started! Let's see just how well you know your Disney favorites by testing how many you can recognize from just two words. Why? Why not? Then match each word pairing to the corresponding emoji.

1. **Wait, what?**

2. **Don't remember**

3. **Can't wait**

4. **Peculiar beauty**

5. **Friend, boot**

6. **Gadgets, bubbles**

7. **Misunderstood, destructive**

8. **Kitty, pigtails**

9. **Hair, magic**

10. **City, crime**

FOR ANSWERS, TURN TO PAGE 110–111 OF THE ANSWER KEY.

# MATCH THE WORD PAIR TO THE DISNEY MOVIE!

Two words: Disney movies. We all know them; we all love them. But how well do *you* know them? Let's find out if you know the Disney movie when you're given just two words as a clue. Match each word pairing to the corresponding emojis on the opposite page.

1. **KITTY, DOOR** ........................................................................

2. **PRIDE, DESTINY** ...................................................................

3. **HAIR, LIGHT** ........................................................................

4. **BALLOON, SQUIRREL** ...........................................................

5. **PARENTS, HOME** .................................................................

6. **SUGAR, SMASH** ...................................................................

7. **DRAGON, SOLDIER** ..............................................................

8. **COWBOY, ALIENS** ...............................................................

9. **UNDER, VOICE** ....................................................................

10. **SHOE, PUMPKIN** .................................................................

# WHAT'S YOUR FAVORITE
## *Tangled* #hashtag?

- #whenwillmylifebegin
- #GOLIVEYOURDREAM
- #Herecomesthesmolder
- #Thugfountain

## WHAT #hashtags
### FOR *TANGLED* CAN YOU COME UP WITH?

#  ............................................................
#  ............................................................
#  ............................................................

#  ............................................................
#  ............................................................
#  ............................................................

ANSWER KEY

# Which Disney Princess Are You?

PAGES 8–17

### IF YOU ANSWERED MOSTLY A . . .

*You're Belle!* You may not always fit in, but your compassionate heart and dreams of adventure will take you far. And yes, that teacup is talking to you.

### IF YOU ANSWERED MOSTLY B . . .

*You're Jasmine!* You're stubborn, energetic, and compassionate. You want to see the world and be allowed to make your own choices. And, may we just say, choosing to wear those harem pants was a pretty great start.

### IF YOU ANSWERED MOSTLY C . . .

*You're Tiana!* You're hardworking, talented, and kind. You're not afraid of rolling up your sleeves and getting the job done, and you're almost there! Disclaimer: not all frogs are princes.

## IF YOU ANSWERED MOSTLY D . . .

 *You're Cinderella!* You never give up on your dreams, and you always remember to be kind to others—even when they haven't always been kind to you. May we suggest wearing heels with a strap to your next ball?

## IF YOU ANSWERED MOSTLY E . . .

 *You're Merida!* You're strong-willed, passionate, and pretty handy with a bow. You're not willing to compromise who you are (or babysit your little brothers). Today just might be the day you change your fate.

## IF YOU ANSWERED MOSTLY F . . .

 *You're Aurora!* You're kind, curious, and eager to explore the world around you. We suggest avoiding spindles.

### IF YOU ANSWERED MOSTLY G . . .

 *You're Rapunzel!* You're creative and optimistic, even in difficult circumstances. You'll never give up on your dreams, and that's the only way to make them come true! So good on you. Just remember to pack your frying pan on your next adventure.

### IF YOU ANSWERED MOSTLY H . . .

 *You're Snow White!* Your big heart and sweet temperament mean you make friends easily. We bet you have at least seven BFFs. Just remember: no mysterious apples for you.

### IF YOU ANSWERED MOSTLY I . . .

 *You're Mulan!* Family is very important to you, but so is being yourself. Luckily, we have a feeling being yourself is exactly what your family wants you to do! All you need is a dragon and a cricket, and you'll be unstoppable.

## IF YOU ANSWERED MOSTLY J . . .

*You're Pocahontas!* You're courageous and open-minded, with an inner strength that's steady as the beating drum. Wherever your compass leads you, you'll be ready for the adventure.

## IF YOU ANSWERED MOSTLY K . . .

*You're Ariel!* You're friendly and fun, with curiosity that will take you on grand adventures. Just don't sign your voice away to an evil sea witch.

## HOW WELL DO YOU KNOW *ALICE IN WONDERLAND?* PAGES 26–31

Question 1: D

Question 2: C

Question 3: A

Question 4: A

Question 5: C

Question 6: D

Question 7: A

Question 8: A

Question 9: C

Question 10: B

Question 11: A

Question 12: B

## DYNAMIC DISNEY DUOS: COMPLETE THEIR CONVERSATIONS! PAGES 32–37

1. Pooch, hospitable

2. Guppy, guppy

3. Disgusting, Calm yourself

4. Sad, strange

102

5. Lost

6. Terrified, friends

7. Left behind

8. It's what friends do

9. Everything's gas

10. Become a human, poor souls

11. Have fun

12. Judgment, true love

## MATCH THE QUOTE TO THE DISNEY DAD! PAGES 42–43

1. Maurice

2. King Triton

3. Mufasa

4. Marlin

5. Zeus

6. Fa Zhou

7. Mr. Incredible

8. Chief Powhatan

9. The Sultan

10. Chief Tui

## MATCH THE DISNEY PRINCESS NAME TO ITS MEANING! PAGES 46–49

1. B
2. C
3. D
4. B
5. A
6. D
7. C
8. A
9. D
10. A
11. B

## THE HARDEST DISNEY•PIXAR QUIZ EVER! PAGES 50–53

1. A

2. False. *Toy Story* was released in 1995.

3. C. Anger says this quote in *Inside Out*.

4. B

5. D

6. A

7. D

8. B

9. D

10. True

11. D

---

## CAN YOU UNSCRAMBLE THE DISNEY VILLAINS' SIDEKICKS' NAMES? PAGES 54–55

1. Pain and Panic

2. Iago

3. Flotsam and Jetsam

4. Sir Hiss

5. The Raven

6. Nero and Brutus

7. Lucifer

8. Percy

## CAN YOU GUESS THE DISNEY CHARACTER AND MOVIE FROM THE TWEET? PAGES 56-59

1. Princess Jasmine or Aladdin, *Aladdin*

2. Princess Ariel, *The Little Mermaid*

3. Anna, *Frozen*

4. Princess Aurora, *Sleeping Beauty*

5. Alice or the Queen of Hearts, *Alice in Wonderland*

6. Belle, *Beauty and the Beast*

7. Simba, *The Lion King*

8. Judy Hopps, *Zootopia*

9. Bambi, Thumper, or Flower, *Bambi*

10. Pinocchio, *Pinocchio*

## ARE YOU THE ULTIMATE DISNEY VILLAIN FAN? PAGES 68-73

1. B

2. A

3. D

4. B

5. B
6. B
7. A
8. B
9. B
10. A
11. C
12. D
13. A
14. D
15. D
16. A
17. A
18. D
19. A
20. B
21. C
22. A
23. D
24. A
25. B

## GUESS THE DISNEY MOVIE BASED ON THE EMOJIS! PAGES 76–77

1. *Finding Nemo*
2. *A Bug's Life*
3. *The Lion King*
4. *Beauty and the Beast*
5. *Hercules*
6. *Lady and the Tramp*
7. *The Little Mermaid*
8. *WALL•E*
9. *Dumbo*
10. *Up*

## UNSCRAMBLE THE DISNEY ANAGRAMS PAGES 78–79

1. "He touched the butt" —Tad
2. "Adventure is out there" —Ellie
3. "You are a toy" —Woody
4. "Just keep swimming" —Dory
5. "So this is love" —Cinderella
6. "'Ohana means family" —Stitch

7. "When you wish upon a star"
—Jiminy Cricket

8. "All it takes is faith and trust" —Peter Pan

9. "I want adventure" —Belle

10. "Change is good" —Rafiki

## CAN YOU GUESS THE DISNEY MOVIE BASED ON THE TAGLINE? PAGES 86–87

1. C

2. A

3. D

4. D

5. C

6. B

7. A

8. D

9. B

10. A

## MATCH THE EMOJI TO THE OVERLY DRAMATIC TITLE PAGES 90–91

1. *Aladdin*

2. *The Lion King*

3. *Beauty and the Beast*

4. *Mulan*

5. *Tangled*

6. *Frozen*

7. *The Little Mermaid*

8. *Hercules*

9. *Sleeping Beauty*

10. *Alice in Wonderland*

## MATCH THE WORD PAIR TO THE DISNEY CHARACTER! PAGES 92–93

1. Anna

2. Dory

3. Simba

4. Belle

5. Woody

6. Ariel

7. Wreck-It Ralph

8. Boo

9. Rapunzel

10. Judy Hopps

---

## MATCH THE WORD PAIR TO THE DISNEY MOVIE! PAGES 94-95

1. *Monsters, Inc.*

2. *The Lion King*

3. *Tangled*

4. *Up*

5. *Finding Dory*

6. *Wreck-It Ralph*

7. *Mulan*

8. *Toy Story*

9. *The Little Mermaid*

10. *Cinderella*